BALLPARK® Mysteries 18 THE ATLANTA ALIBI

BALLPARK MYSTERIES®

The MVP Series

BALLPARK Mysteries 18
THE ATLANTA ALIBI

by David A. Kelly

illustrated by Mark Meyers

A STEPPING STONE BOOK™

Random House 🏠 New York

This book is dedicated to my younger self. As a kid, I struggled to read. I hated to write. And I didn't know much about baseball. But because I worked hard, listened to my teachers and editors, and never gave up, I have managed to write twenty-two Ballpark Mysteries books.
—D.A.K.

Roberta, John, Jinna, Sarah, and Taline—
it has been wonderful playing on your team!
—M.M.

"The way I see it, it's a great thing to be the man who hit the most home runs, but it's a greater thing to be the man who does the most with the home runs he hits."
—Hank Aaron

Library of Congress Cataloging-in-Publication Data
Names: Kelly, David A. (David Andrew), author. | Meyers, Mark, illustrator. | Kelly, David A. (David Andrew), Ballpark mysteries; 18.
Title: The Atlanta alibi / by David A. Kelly; illustrated by Mark Meyers.
Description: New York: Random House Children's Books, 2022. | Series: Ballpark mysteries; 18 | "A Stepping Stone book."
Summary: When cousins Mike and Kate discover that the bat and ball that Hank Aaron used to hit his 715th home run have gone missing from the Atlanta Braves ballpark, apparently by someone who wants the Braves' manager fired—Mike and Kate are determined to solve the mystery and get the stolen artifacts back.
Identifiers: LCCN 2021005570 | ISBN 978-0-593-12627-1 (trade pbk.) | ISBN 978-0-593-12628-8 (lib. bdg.) | ISBN 978-0-593-12629-5 (ebook)
Subjects: LCSH: Atlanta Braves (Baseball team)—History—Juvenile literature. | Baseball stories. | Theft—Juvenile fiction. | Cousins—Juvenile fiction. | Detective and mystery stories. | Atlanta (Ga.)—Juvenile fiction. | CYAC: Atlanta Braves (Baseball team)—Fiction. | Baseball—Fiction. | Stealing—Fiction. | Cousins—Fiction. | Atlanta (Ga.)—Fiction. | Mystery and detective stories. | LCGFT: Detective and mystery fiction.
Classification: LCC PZ7.K2936 At 2022 | DDC 813.6 [Fic]—dc23

Printed in the United States of America
10 9 8 7 6 5 4 3 2 1

Contents

Hammerin' Hank

"Uh-oh, another bad call!" Mike Walsh said to his cousin Kate Hopkins. "Watch this. Tommy's going to explode!"

The Atlanta Braves' manager, Tommy Blocks, shot out of the team's dugout. The Braves were two runs behind the Boston Red Sox in the eighth inning. Even though it was close, the umpire had just called the Braves' Pete Uker out at first.

Tommy ran over to the first-base umpire

and started yelling. He pointed at Pete and waved his arms wildly. "Are you even paying attention?" he cried. "He was safe! Like a bank. Go back to Little League!"

The umpire stepped closer to Tommy. "Out! He was out!" the umpire called. "And you will be, too, if you keep it up!"

Tommy waved his arms at first base. "Wake up, ump," he shouted. Tommy glanced at his team in the dugout. "Hey! Look, guys, the circus is in town and the clowns are wearing blue!"

The Atlanta fans cheered and whistled.

The umpire leaned closer to Tommy. "That's it!" he said. "I'm the umpire. You're the one acting like a clown!"

"Well, get out your little broom, then," Tommy said. "Because you're going to need to clean up your act!"

Tommy stepped back and started kicking the dirt. Clouds of dust flew onto the umpire's shoes and pants.

The crowd stood and exploded with cheers.

The umpire looked down at the swirls of dirt hitting his legs. Then he threw his arm out and pointed to the stands.

"YOU'RE OUT OF THE GAME!" the umpire yelled. "NOW!"

Tommy stopped kicking at the ground. He puffed his chest out and bumped into the umpire. A small smile crossed his face. "Oh, I'm going," he said. "But I'll be back!"

Tommy kicked one last cloud of dust and disappeared down the stairs into the Atlanta locker room.

The fans cheered.

"That's the one hundred and sixty-first time Tommy's been thrown out of a game!" Mike said. "It's the most for any major-league manager! He says it gets the team fired up and helps them win."

"Well, it may help them win," Kate said,

"but I don't know if he's making any friends acting like that!"

It was a Thursday night in May, and Kate and Mike were in Atlanta, Georgia, at an Atlanta Braves baseball game. They had flown down from their home in Cooperstown, New York, earlier that day with Kate's mom. She worked as a sports reporter and was covering the weekend series between the Braves and the Boston Red Sox. Mrs. Hopkins was working up in the press box. Kate and Mike had seats near the Braves dugout.

"I hope Big D will be in tomorrow's game," Mike said. "Maybe we can wave to him on the field!"

Big D was Mike and Kate's friend and the star hitter on the Boston Red Sox. He was sitting out tonight's game because of an injury.

"I'm sure he will be," Kate said. She pointed

to the wide-mouth cup Mike was holding. "How are those boiled peanuts?" she asked. "They're a Southern specialty."

Mike dipped his finger in the container of wet peanuts and stirred them around. "Well," he said, "it's a little weird that they're soft. But I like them, because they *are* salty!"

Mike put the cup on the ground and pulled a baseball out from the pocket of his hooded sweatshirt. He had bought the ball earlier that night. It was a special Henry "Hank" Aaron edition, with the famous hitter's signature printed on it. Mike tossed it from hand to hand.

"I can't wait to try this ball on the field at home," he said. "Since it's a Hank Aaron ball, I bet I can hit it a mile!"

"Maybe you can compare it to Hank's famous home run ball tomorrow afternoon," Kate said. She pointed to the rows of seats above left field. "My mom arranged a private tour of the Hank Aaron Terrace up there before the game. We'll get to see the ball and bat that Hammerin' Hank used to hit home run number seven hundred and fifteen to beat Babe Ruth's home run record!"

"Cool!" Mike said as he dropped the baseball in his lap. He clenched his hands and pretended to swing a bat. "Pow! Hammerin' Hank versus me, the Sultan of Swat! Wait until *I* get up to bat! Then we'll really see who's the King of Swing!"

Kate rolled her eyes and checked the scoreboard. The Braves were still behind by two, and it was the ninth inning.

"Well, the Braves could really use one of

you," Kate said. "Hammerin' Hank or Moon-Shot Mike. They need at least three runs to win."

But unfortunately, the Braves didn't have anyone like that on their team tonight. When they got up to bat, one hitter after another struck out. Three up. Three down. The Braves had lost. Tommy's outburst against the umpire hadn't worked.

As they stood up to leave, Mike started searching around. He lifted the seat and looked underneath it.

"Hey, Kate, hang on a minute," Mike said. "My Hank Aaron baseball is missing!"

A Swing and a Miss

"Really?" Kate asked. "Where could it be?"

Mike dropped to his knees and scanned the cement floor. "I don't know," he said. "I had it a while ago."

Kate looked at Mike and started laughing.

"Hey, this isn't funny!" Mike said. As his face started to turn red, his freckles stood out even more. "I just bought that ball tonight!"

"Well then, let me help you," Kate said. She reached over Mike's shoulder and pulled the hood of his sweatshirt up over his head. As she did, something dropped out.

BONK!

"Ouch!" Mike said as he jumped to the side.

BOING!

His Hank Aaron baseball bounced on the ground!

Kate laughed as Mike scooped his ball up. "You left it on the floor earlier," she said. "I thought you'd forget it, so I secretly slipped it into your hood. That way I knew you wouldn't lose it!"

"Thanks a *lot*!" Mike said.

"No problem, cuz," Kate said. "Happy to help! Come on, let's go find my mom!"

*****

The next day, Mike, Kate, and Mrs. Hopkins arrived at the Braves stadium in the middle of the afternoon. It was hours until that night's game, but they had arrived early for a tour of the Hank Aaron Terrace.

Ahead of them was the Braves Monument Garden, an area with exhibits of Braves retired numbers, Gold Glove Awards, Silver Slugger Awards, different Braves jerseys, and Braves history. Large pictures of famous Braves players hung along the edge of the monument area, and a rustle of voices rose from a crowd on the far side.

"Oh, cool!" Mike said. "Monument Garden! But why is there a crowd?"

"The Braves are having a party for Tommy Blocks to celebrate his twenty-fifth year of managing the Braves," Mrs. Hopkins said. "They invited us reporters, and I thought you might enjoy stopping by before our tour. Some of the baseball players from the Braves and the Red Sox will be here, and, of course, Tommy Blocks. In fact, he's right over there." She pointed to a group standing next to a life-size Hank Aaron statue.

"Woo-hoo!" Mike said. He pulled out a marker and his baseball. "Even though he's a bit of a bully, maybe I can get him to sign this! Come on, Kate."

"Thanks, Mom!" Kate said. She gave her mother a hug and took off after Mike.

Mike and Kate ran up the Monument Garden walkway. At the top was a large bronze statue of Hank Aaron slugging home run number 715, the one that beat Babe Ruth's famous record. Behind the statue stood a sculpture of the number 715 made from 715 baseball bats. Each bat represented one of Hank's home runs.

A small group huddled around manager Tommy Blocks. Mike and Kate stepped up

to listen as Tommy joked with the crowd. A broad-shouldered man in front of Mike and Kate had just poured a few red gummy candies from a yellow bag into his palm.

"This is my first-base coach, 'Smarty' Marty Miller," Tommy said. He glanced at Marty's candy. "He's got a sweet tooth, but I call him 'Smarty' because he thinks he knows everything!"

Marty smiled. "Aww, Tommy, you know I think you're great," he said as he popped a few candies in his mouth. "But if you ever want to take a break from coaching and retire, let me know and I'd be happy to fill in for you!"

"Oh, thanks, Marty," Tommy said. He pointed over his shoulder. "Hey, can y'all watch my back?" he said as he jabbed Marty lightly in the ribs. "This guy would take me out if he thought he could get my job. I know you're just hoping I'll retire so you can be coach. Sorry, Smarty, but not a chance!"

Marty smiled and bowed slightly. "Just trying to help, Tommy," he said. "Don't get excited."

"That's *not* the type of help that I need," Tommy said. He jabbed a finger at a compact man with sharp blue eyes, neatly combed hair, and a trim beard.

"Oliver, you used to be an umpire! I know you didn't always agree with me, but I'd still love to have you back out there as plate umpire. I need umpires that see things *my way*."

Oliver cracked a tight smile. "Thanks, Tommy," he said slowly. "But maybe if you didn't give umpires such a hard time, they'd go along with you a bit more. We don't want to fight. We just want to call 'em like we see 'em."

Oliver patted Tommy on the shoulder.

"It's nice to be retired so I don't have to make calls that get you upset," he said. "But maybe it *is* time for you to consider retirement, like Marty said!"

"Ah! It always comes back to Marty and my retirement, doesn't it?" Tommy roared. "I *told* you he was after my job!"

Tommy slapped Marty on the back and gave a big laugh. A few moments later, the group broke up and people moved on.

Mike stepped forward and held out his baseball and marker. "Would you please sign my ball, Mr. Blocks?" he asked. "I'm Mike Walsh, and this is my cousin Kate."

"Sure," Tommy said with a smile. "As long as you don't grow up to be umpires. Or first-base coaches!"

"Nope," Kate said as Tommy signed the baseball. "Mike's going to be a baseball hitter like Hank Aaron or Big D, and I'm going to be a veterinarian."

"Thanks for the autograph," Mike said to Tommy. "We've got to get going, but good luck tonight!"

Tommy nodded and waved goodbye.

Kate and Mike ran over to Mrs. Hopkins. She was standing near an elevator on the other side of the hallway. With her was Oliver, the retired umpire who had been joking with Tommy.

"Mike, Kate, this is Oliver," Mrs. Hopkins said as they arrived. "He's going to give us a tour of the Hank Aaron Terrace. He used to be a major-league umpire, but now he works part-time as a historian for the Braves."

"Nice to meet you," Oliver said. "I'm happy to share some Hank Aaron memories with you." Oliver ushered them into the elevator. "Hank was one of the all-time great baseball players. He played for the Braves for twenty-one seasons and held the career home run record for thirty-three years, taking it over from Babe Ruth in 1974 right here in Atlanta. He still holds the records for most runs batted in, extra base hits, and total bases even though he retired in 1976!"

The elevator stopped, and the doors opened into a large restaurant area with windows overlooking the field. A huge Hank Aaron bobblehead stood just to their right.

Mike jumped over to the huge Hank. "Hey, Kate, come here and say cheese!" he said.

Mrs. Hopkins took pictures of Mike and Kate standing next to the bobblehead, first a serious one and then a picture of Kate and Mike pretending to swing a home run. When they were done, Oliver pointed to one of the columns in the middle of the floor.

"Hank loved Atlanta so much that he wanted the baseball and his bat from that historic seven hundred and fifteenth home run to stay here with the Braves rather than go to the Baseball Hall of Fame in Cooperstown,"

Oliver said. "So the Braves put them on display right here at the ballpark. They're worth a huge amount of money." He gestured to a glass display case mounted in the column.

Mike and Kate crowded forward to see the famous treasures. As they stepped up to the glass case, they looked at each other and then back at the case.

"Um, Oliver?" Kate said.

"Yes?" Oliver said.

"It looks like Hank Aaron's ball and bat are missing!"

A Tough Choice

"What?" Oliver said. He bounded over.

Kate was right. Hank Aaron's famous 715th home run ball and bat were gone. The case behind the glass panel was empty!

"Oh no!" Oliver said. He pushed on the glass. It didn't budge. He checked the special screws around the edges. They were tight.

"There's no sign of any damage," Oliver said. "I don't know how anyone could have stolen them! I've got to call Jamal, our head of security!"

Oliver pulled his phone out and made a call. When he was done, he slipped the phone back into his pocket. "Jamal used to be a detective with the Atlanta police," he said. "If anyone can find a thief, he can! And if he can't, he'll get the police involved."

Kate moved closer to the glass and pushed up on her tiptoes.

"And what's that?" she asked. "At the bottom of the case?"

Mike, Oliver, and Mrs. Hopkins leaned in to see what Kate was talking about.

"It looks like a note," Mike said.

"Let's wait for Jamal to check it out," Oliver said. "He'll be here shortly."

As Kate's mom took a phone call for work, Mike whispered to Kate, "Whoever stole Hank's bat and ball may have left some clues. Let's look while we have time!"

Kate nodded. "Good idea," she said. She scanned the long room. It was filled with dining tables and chairs. A food-and-drink counter stood in the middle. There were Exit signs above doors at both ends. One whole side of the room was made of plate-glass windows that looked down on the field.

Kate pointed to a table not far away. There was a popcorn machine on it. "Let's start there," she said. "Maybe that's where the thief put his tools down or left something behind."

Mike and Kate raced over to the table. The large glass-walled popcorn machine was empty, so they searched the floor.

Just then, a man and a woman dressed in blue security shirts entered the room. The man was carrying a black bag.

"Jamal, Kayla, over here," Oliver said. "Hank's ball and bat have been stolen!"

"This is terrible," Jamal said. He set the black bag down next to the display case, and Mike, Kate, and Mrs. Hopkins walked over.

"We'll dust for prints," Kayla said as she examined the glass. "How do we open the case?"

Oliver pointed to a silver keyhole on the bottom. "You need a key," he said. "It's kept in the safe in the front office. Only Taylor Turner, the team owner, has the combination to the safe. But since I'm the team historian, I have access to it once a year to make sure the items are okay."

Jamal nodded. "We'll follow up with Mr. Turner to see if anyone else has used the key recently," he said. "Oliver, can you go get it now so we can dust for prints?"

"Sure! I'm on my way," Oliver said as he hustled to the door.

Jamal and Kayla put rubber gloves on.

Then Jamal took out a fluffy brush and a container of black powder.

Kate nudged Mike. "We've never seen anyone dust for fingerprints for real!" she said.

"Nope, you're right," Mike said. "But I read about how Jigsaw Jones did it in the glow-in-the-dark ghost mystery I got from the school library last month. This will be cool!"

Jamal dipped the brush in the container and swirled it around. Then he started to gently sweep the brush around the edges of the display case glass.

Not much happened at first. But then something did!

"Whoa! Look at that!" Mike said. "Fingerprints!"

Most of the glass was clean, but in a few areas, small black specks of powder had stuck to the glass.

"Looks like we have three," Jamal said. "This thief is as good as caught!"

"Wow, that's cool!" Kate said. "They look perfect!"

Kayla picked up a roll of clear tape from the bag. She cut off a few pieces and then pressed the sticky part against the powdered fingerprints. "Got 'em!" she said. She lifted the strips of tape and placed them on small white note cards.

"Good work!" Jamal said. "We can run them through our security system. We have the fingerprints of everyone who works here on file."

As Jamal was finishing up, Oliver returned. He held a long silver key. "Got it!" he said.

"When's the last time you took the cover off?" Jamal asked Oliver.

"Oh, I don't know," Oliver replied. "About

six months ago. I do it once a year to inspect the items. We do that with all our exhibits."

Oliver reached down and slipped the key into the lock at the bottom of the case. The lock made a loud click when he turned it. Then he pulled the glass cover away.

The case was completely empty except for a small silver baseball holder at the bottom where Hank Aaron's 715th home run baseball should have been. Instead, there was a folded note on it.

Jamal quickly dusted the inside of the case for prints. "Zip," he said. "No fingerprints on the inside of the case."

With that, Kayla reached in and pulled the piece of paper out. As she did, a small red gummy fish fell to the floor!

"What's that?" Jamal asked.

Kayla picked up the candy fish.

"Looks like a Little Red Herring to me!" Mike said. "Next to Gummy Sharks, those are one of my favorite foods!"

Kayla nodded and dropped the candy into an evidence bag.

"Now, what about that note?" Jamal asked.

Kayla unfolded it.

The note was handwritten in dark blue pen. It read:

Tommy has had his last tantrum.
If you don't throw Tommy out of the game for good, you'll never see Hank's ball and bat again!

Little Red Herrings

"Whoa! Someone wants Tommy gone *really* badly," Kate said.

"Stealing Hank Aaron's treasures is just wrong," Jamal said. "They mean so much to the fans!"

"I know," Oliver said. "We've got to get Hank's bat and ball back, no matter what!"

Mike pointed to the note. "Look at the top," he said. The team logo, a swirly capital *A* for Atlanta, was printed across the top of the paper. "Maybe someone from the team is the thief!"

Oliver nodded. "You're right," he said. "That's from one of our standard notepads. Anyone with the team, like a player or even a coach, could have written that!"

"We'll definitely check it out!" Kayla said. She dropped the note into an evidence collection bag. "Jamal, let's head back to the office so we can analyze those fingerprints."

"We'll contact you once we have some information, Oliver," Jamal said. "You should check on the other artifacts around the stadium to see if anything else is missing. We'll keep an eye on Tommy."

Jamal and Kayla packed up their black bag and left.

Oliver looked at his watch. "Time for us to go, too," he said. "The game will start in about an hour. We might as well watch Tommy coach the Braves for the last time."

* * * * *

A little while later, Mike and Kate were back in the hallway near the Braves Monument Garden. Oliver had set off to check on the other team artifacts, while Mrs. Hopkins had given Mike and Kate some money for dinner and had gone to the pressroom for the game.

"We've got to go to bat for Hank!" Mike said as he and Kate headed down a walkway to the field. "Let's figure out where his missing stuff is!"

Kate nodded. "I know," she said. "I've been thinking about the suspects."

Mike and Kate emerged from the walkway to an area overlooking the field. Fans streamed by on either side of them.

"Whoever took Hank's things had the motive, the means, and the opportunity," Kate said. On the flight down to Atlanta, she had been reading a book about solving crimes. She loved to read. "The *motive* is wanting the team to get rid of Tommy. The *means* is having the key to open the display case."

"And the *opportunity* is the chance to commit the crime!" Mike said. "Whoever did it must have had access to that room before or after games."

"Exactly. We're looking for someone who has a grudge against Tommy, who could get the key, and who could be in the stadium when it's not busy," Kate said.

Mike's eyes were drawn to some activity down on the field. The grounds crew was raking the infield dirt. Over to the side, the first-base umpire from the previous day's game was looking at the field.

Mike stared at him for a moment. Then he nodded slightly and smiled.

"I think I know someone who had the motive and the opportunity!" he said.

"Who?" Kate asked.

Mike pointed to the side of the field. "The umpire!" he said. "The first-base umpire from yesterday is probably tired of being yelled at by Tommy, so he wants to get rid of him!"

Kate watched the umpire walk from first

base to home plate. "Maybe," she said. "He certainly has a reason, or the motive, to want Tommy gone."

"And the opportunity," Mike said. "Nobody would question him if he were hanging around before or after games. He probably just waited for the stadium to empty out yesterday."

"Or he came in early this morning," Kate added.

"And then stole the ball and bat somehow," Mike said. "It fits perfectly!"

"Since the display case glass wasn't broken, he'd need a key like the one Oliver has. That's the means," Kate said. "Maybe he has a key in the umpire's room with his stuff. Let's go see if we can find it!"

They dashed back into the stadium's main walkway. It was even more crowded now. There were hundreds of kids hanging around. Some wore brightly colored baseball uniforms. Others were in shorts and T-shirts.

Mike skidded to a halt as he looked around. "What's going on?" he asked.

"I don't know," Kate said. "It looks like a bunch of Little League baseball teams lined up for something!"

The line stretched on and on. Just as Mike and Kate were passing a group of players dressed in blue-and-white jerseys, a voice called out from behind them.

"Mike! Kate!"

Kate and Mike spun around. A boy in a baseball jersey stepped out of the crowd and waved his hands.

"It's Polo!" Kate said. "From the Little League World Series team!"

Mike and Kate had met Polo when they were in Williamsport, Pennsylvania, for the

Little League World Series. They had been cheering on the Cooperstown, New York, team but had become friends with some of the players on other teams. Polo was on the Southeast Regional team from Georgia.

Mike and Kate ran over to Polo. He was a tall, thin boy with dark hair. He gave them each a fist bump.

"Wow! What are you two doing in Atlanta?" he asked. "This is so cool!"

"I know!" Mike said. "We're here with Kate's mom, watching the game. What are you doing?"

Polo nodded at the nearby kids with baseball gloves and balls. "I'm here with my team," he said. "The Braves invite Little League teams to walk around the warning track before home games."

"You get to go on the field before the game?" Mike asked. "That's awesome!"

Polo gave Mike a high-five. "Yes, it is!" he said. "And I've got an idea. How'd you like to come with us?"

"Really?" Kate asked. "How could we do that?"

"Simple," Polo said. "Just hang with me and pretend you're part of our team. I'll let Coach Waleed know. He won't mind."

"Sounds great!" Mike said. "Let's go! We can imagine we're walking on for a position in tonight's game!"

"Or maybe we can keep an eye on the umpire," Kate whispered to Mike as they blended in with Polo's team.

A few minutes later, the long line of kids started moving. Kate, Mike, and Polo followed the groups ahead of them through the stadium and then finally out onto the warning track at the left-field foul pole.

Mike and Kate looked up at the tens of

thousands of fans cheering in the stands. Mike instantly started waving and taking bows as if he were a famous baseball pitcher walking out to save the game. Then he turned to some of the kids on Polo's team and asked them for the baseballs they were carrying.

"Hey, Kate, watch this!" Mike said. "I'm the famous baseball juggler!"

Mike tossed a baseball up into the air. Then he threw a second and third one. The balls continued to fly up and down between Mike's hands as he walked.

A moment later, as Mike stepped across home plate, a huge smile crossed his face. "I'm juggling!" he said. "It's another home run for the baseball juggler!"

"That's amazing, Mike," Kate said. She borrowed a baseball from one of Polo's teammates. "Here, try one more!"

"No!" Mike called out. "Not four! I can only juggle three!"

But it was too late! Kate had already tossed the baseball to Mike. He grabbed it and tossed it up in the air. Polo and his teammates watched as Mike juggled the four baseballs for a few seconds.

But then Mike sneezed! His whole body shook, and a ball slipped through his fingers and hit the ground. The other balls landed near the Atlanta dugout with three thuds.

Polo laughed. "I'd call that four passed balls!" he said as he and the team started to walk again.

Mike pretended to tip his hat and scurried off to the grass in front of the dugout to pick up the balls. A moment later, he was back. "Take a look at that," Mike said. He pointed to the dugout.

Smarty Marty, the Braves' first-base coach, was standing at the railing overlooking the field. He was just a few feet away and close enough for Kate to easily see the yellow candy wrapper in his right hand and the red spots in his left hand.

Kate looked back at Mike. Her eyes were opened wide.

"He's eating . . . ," Kate said.

"Little Red Herrings!" Mike said.

Captured

"Maybe Smarty Marty stole Hank's bat and ball!" Kate said to Mike as they continued down the warning track to a door.

Mike nodded and clicked off the facts on his fingers. "One, he's eating the food we found at the crime scene. Two, we know he loves candy. And three, Tommy said that Marty really wants to take his job!"

"That's the motive!" Kate said. "And he has the opportunity. No one would suspect him hanging around the stadium while he waited for the perfect time."

After passing through a gate in right field, Mike and Kate found themselves standing in a hallway underneath the stands.

"I've got to go with the team to our seats," Polo said. "But it was great seeing you!"

"You too!" Kate said. "Thanks for letting us tag along!"

"Maybe we'll see you again at the Little League World Series next year," Mike said.

Polo smiled. "If I can find my home run groove, you sure will!" he said, and waved goodbye.

Kate turned around and gave Mike's shirt a quick tug. "Come on," she said. "We should tell Oliver what we found out about Smarty Marty! Let's go to his office first. Maybe he's there!"

Mike and Kate raced through the stadium until they were back on the main walkway. They headed for the stairs to the lower level, where a security guard stopped them.

"Hold up there," she said. "Where are you two headed in such a hurry?"

"We're trying to find Oliver," Mike said. "We were with him earlier today and have some important information for him. Can you tell us where his office is?"

The security guard studied Mike and Kate for a moment, and then she turned and spoke into her radio. A moment later, it buzzed and a voice said: "All clear!"

The guard stepped aside. "Oliver said to send you down to his office," she said. "Turn left at the bottom of the stairs. Room B-243."

Mike and Kate raced down the stairs and through the hallway. They passed food vendors stocking up their trays and workers zooming by on electric carts.

When they reached Oliver's office, Kate

knocked on the door. A moment later, Oliver opened it.

"Oh, hi," he said. "It's you two. You can stop by anytime. I just got back from checking on the other artifacts. Nothing else is missing, from what I can tell. I can't believe that Hank's ball and bat were stolen!"

Kate nodded. "That's why we're here," she said. "We might have a clue."

"Really?" Oliver asked. "Come in!"

The small room was filled with plaques, trophies, magazine articles, gloves, and other baseball equipment. Giant signed posters of Hank Aaron hitting home run number 715 lined one wall. A large rack filled with cardboard poster tubes stood in front of the wall. They were labeled AUTOGRAPHED BY HANK AARON.

"Wow!" Mike said. "Are those posters all signed by Hank Aaron?"

Oliver nodded. "They are," he said. "And you can both take one if you want. We keep a bunch of extras around to give out to VIPs. Go ahead and choose two from that rack!"

"Thanks!" Mike and Kate said in unison.

Mike grabbed the one nearest to him. He picked it up. It was light and long. Mike tossed it to Kate. "Quick, catch!" he said. "It's a Hank Aaron hit to deep center!"

Kate didn't miss a beat. She snagged the poster tube as it flew by. "And it's caught by Kate Hopkins for an out!" she said. "Better luck next time, Hank!"

"Thanks," Mike said. "That was a nice catch!"

As he reached for another poster tube, Mike spotted one off to the side. He snatched it with his right hand. Mike tried to toss it to his left hand so he could catch it just like Kate did, but the tube clunked to the floor with a thud. Oliver hustled over and picked it up.

"Oh, not that one," Oliver said. "I had set that aside for a project I'm working on." He leaned the tube against his desk and used a marker to write SAVE across the top. Then he pointed to the poster tubes in front of the pile. "Just take one of those."

Mike took another poster tube with his right hand and tossed it. This time, he caught it easily in his other hand.

"Bingo," he said. "Two outs for Hank! One more and the inning will be over!"

Oliver checked his watch. "Now, why did you need to see me so urgently?" he asked.

Mike pointed at the posters on the wall. "Hank's missing ball and bat," he said. "We were just down on the field with the Little League teams, and Kate spotted something important."

"What?" Oliver asked.

"We passed by the Atlanta dugout," Kate said. "And we saw Smarty Marty eating Little Red Herrings! Just like the one we found in the case!"

"We also know that Tommy was worried that Marty wanted his job," Mike said. "Since Marty is a coach, he probably has access to that room after hours, and no one would suspect him!"

"And he would have access to those team notepads, too," Kate said.

Oliver nodded. "Wow," he said. "That makes a lot of sense. I'd hate to think that Marty did it, but you're right, it probably *was* someone close to the team. We need to tell Jamal."

Oliver used the office phone to call Jamal. They talked for a minute and then hung up.

"Jamal said he was on his way here anyway," Oliver said. "He should be here in a few minutes."

Oliver started leafing through a notebook on his desk. "All the other important team artifacts seem to be in order," he said. "We have to get Hank's stuff back, even if that means Tommy has to go!"

"That would be terrible," Mike said as he approached the desk. "Hopefully, Jamal and Kayla can match those fingerprints."

"Or investigate Smarty Marty," Kate said. "It seems like there are a lot of clues to work with!"

Oliver sighed. "I guess you're right," he said.

Something on the desk caught Mike's eye. He leaned over and pointed to a small pad of paper.

"Hey, that's one of the official Atlanta notepads you mentioned," Mike said. "Could we have a page of it to study? Maybe we can get Smarty Marty to write his autograph on it, and we can compare it to the writing on the note we found!"

Oliver glanced at the pad. "Oh, that?" he asked. He picked the pad up and turned it over in his hands. "Sure. In fact, you can have the whole thing," he said. "I've got a pile of them in my drawer."

Oliver tossed the pad to Mike. "Here, you might as well have a team pencil, too," he said as he slid a pencil with the team logo across the desk.

"Thanks!" Mike said. He picked up the pencil. "Even if it doesn't help us find Hank's ball and bat, I could always use it to write down some lineups for the team."

Just then, there was a knock at the door. It opened. Jamal and Kayla stepped in. They smiled at Mike and Kate but headed for Oliver.

"Oliver, I'm afraid you're going to have to come with us," Kayla said. "We identified the person who left the fingerprints!"

"Wow! That's great!" Oliver said. He flashed a broad smile. "Good work! Mike and Kate have some information for you. If you've solved the mystery, why do you need me?"

Kayla crossed her arms. "Well, we'd like to know if you have anything you want to tell us," she said.

"Me?" Oliver said. He brushed his hair back with one hand. "No, I don't have any-thing to say. I thought you wanted to tell *me* something."

"We've been studying the evidence," Kayla said. "And it leads us to just one question. Did *you* take Hank's ball and bat?"

One Last Game

"The three fingerprints we lifted at the scene of the crime were yours," Kayla said.

"But I'm not a thief!" Oliver said.

Kate stepped forward. "Hang on a minute," she said. Kate turned to Kayla. "You didn't find any fingerprints on the inside of the case, right?"

Kayla nodded. "Yes, that's right," she said.

"But Oliver's fingerprints matched the ones you found on the outside of the case?" she asked.

"Yes, exactly," Kayla said.

"I don't think that means Oliver stole the bat and ball," Kate said. "When we first found them missing, Oliver put his fingers all over the glass case to test it and see if it was secure. Mike and I were there! The ball and bat were already missing. The fingerprints you found were from when we were with him! We saw him touch the case."

Kayla and Jamal looked at Oliver for a moment.

"Okay, that makes sense," Kayla said. "We didn't *really* think that Oliver would steal Hank's ball and bat, but we have to follow up on every possibility."

Oliver leaned against his desk. "Thank you, Kate!" he said. "I'm *not* a thief."

"We know that," Kate said.

"But we also know who might be!" Mike said.

Kayla and Jamal turned and looked at Mike. "Who?" they asked.

"Smarty Marty!" Mike said.

Mike and Kate explained their deduction and how they saw Marty eating the Little Red Herrings in the dugout.

"That sounds like a good lead," Jamal said. "Thanks. We'll follow up on it and get back to you, although we may have to wait until after the game." He handed Kate a business card. "If you hear or see anything else, please give us a call."

"Have you found any other leads?" Oliver asked.

"We interviewed the cleaning staff, and they verified that the bat and ball were still there last night at eleven p.m.," Kayla said. "So we know the theft happened after that."

Oliver nodded. "Well, good luck!" he said.

Jamal and Kayla went to the door. "We'll be in touch if we find out anything else," Jamal said.

Oliver smiled and waved. "Sounds good," he said.

Jamal and Kayla left. Oliver looked at his watch. "Well, thanks for saving me!" he said. "I guess I owe you one. How'd you like to join some friends of the team and sit *directly* behind the right fielder at *field level*? You'll be so close you can talk to him! The team is hosting a group tonight."

"Wow!" Mike said. "That's cool! You mean we'd be right behind the warning track?"

"Yup," Oliver said. "Exactly! Usually the seats are only available for groups, but I can get you in today."

"We'd love to, but I have to check with my mom," Kate said. She called her mother and explained Oliver's offer. After Kate's mom talked to Oliver, she gave her approval.

A short time later, Mike and Kate were sitting just inches from the outfield! They had set their poster tubes down against the strong wire fence in front of them, which separated the seating area from the right-field warning track. They could smell the fresh-cut grass just feet away. It was the top of the first inning, and the Boston Red Sox were batting.

"This is unbelievable!" Mike said. "Look, Big D's up!"

The Red Sox already had two outs against them. But Big D was one of Boston's best hitters and good friends with Mike and Kate. They had helped him find his stolen baseball bat at Fenway Park. Big D strode up to the plate and took some practice swings. He adjusted his helmet and stared at the Atlanta pitcher. The hometown crowd was cheering wildly.

The Atlanta pitcher fired a curveball at the plate.

Big D lifted his front leg and stepped forward while taking a huge swing.

CRAAAAACK!

The bat made a splintering noise as the ball bounced high into the sky.

Big D looked at the bat for a moment. It was still in one piece. Then he dropped the bat and ran for first. The ball flew toward right field, but it was short.

"Oh no, his bat must have cracked!" Mike said.

"But it didn't break apart," Kate said.

Mike nodded. "Sometimes that happens," he said.

The Braves fielder was running back to the warning track in front of Kate and Mike. When he was about five feet away, the fielder reached his glove up, and Big D's baseball dropped into it. Mike and Kate were close enough to touch the fielder.

The crowd cheered. The Braves jogged off the field. The Red Sox players ran out to their positions.

"Awwww, that's too bad for Big D!" Mike said.

"But it's good for Atlanta," Kate said. "They *are* the hometown team!"

"You cheer for them, and I'll cheer for Big D," Mike said. He reached forward and grabbed the metal fence. He gave it a shake. "Now, if only this was a little looser, I could sneak out there and help the Red Sox with their fielding. . . ."

"I don't think you'll need to," Kate said. "Look!"

Mike glanced up.

"It's Big D!" he said. "He's playing right field! We can say hi!"

Big D was jogging to the outfield. When he reached deep right field, he stopped and turned to face home plate.

"Big D! Big D!" Mike and Kate called.

Big D turned around and scanned the stands.

"Down here!" Kate called.

Big D lowered his eyes, and then his face broke into a friendly smile.

"Mike and Kate!" he called. "My two favorite detectives. Give me some good luck!" He quickly jogged over. He held his glove up against the metal fence as Mike and Kate gave him fist bumps through it.

"You two trying to see what it's like to play right field?" Big D asked.

"Naw," Mike said with a smile. "We're just keeping an eye on you! What happened with that hit?"

Big D shook his head. "The bat cracked," he said. "Otherwise I would have had a home run. How'd you two like it as a souvenir? Kate, I'll give it to your mother after the game."

"That sounds like a home run to me," Kate said.

"I'd love to stay and chat, but I'm afraid I've got a baseball game to play," Big D said. "I'll see you later!" He tipped his Red Sox hat and ran back to his position.

The second half of the first inning went slowly. Atlanta players got one base hit after another. By the time three outs were up, Atlanta had three runs!

Big D waved to Mike and Kate. Then he sprinted to the Boston dugout.

Just as Atlanta took the field for the second inning, Oliver stopped by Mike and Kate's seats.

"Pretty good seats, right?" he asked with a smile.

"Not really," Mike said.

Oliver's smile drooped. "They're not?" he asked.

Mike shook his head. "Nope," he said. "They're GREAT!"

Oliver laughed. "Good one," he said. "Now, sit back and enjoy the night, because I just found out that this is going to be Tommy Blocks's last game!"

A New Manager

The next day, Mike, Kate, and Mrs. Hopkins spent the morning at the Martin Luther King Jr. Birthplace Historical Park, in downtown Atlanta. They had seen a movie about the famous civil rights leader, looked through a museum dedicated to him, and taken a tour of the house where he was born.

"That was pretty incredible," Mike said. "Martin Luther King Jr. was an amazing person!"

"He was," Kate said. "But did you know

that he was actually born Michael King Jr.? His father renamed him Martin Luther when he was five, in honor of a famous priest."

"I didn't know that," Mike said. "But I know I would want him on my team!"

"Well, you know who else was on his team?" Kate asked.

"No, who?" Mike asked.

"Hank Aaron!" Kate said. "Follow me. We need to find something I read about in my guidebook."

Kate guided Mike and her mom past the museum entrance to a sidewalk that led to the parking lot. She scanned the concrete squares until she spotted something. Then she ran a few steps ahead, planted her feet firmly on the sidewalk, and pretended to swing a baseball bat.

"What are you doing?" Mike asked.

Kate took a step back and pointed to the

ground. "Look, it's Hank Aaron's footprints!" she said. "They put the footprints of famous people who fought for civil rights into this Walk of Fame."

Set into the sidewalk was a large square of gray stone with the name Henry Aaron carved into it. In the middle were two black stone footprints outlined with a shallow edge.

"Hey, that gives me an idea," Mike said. "Let's get Big D's bat, and then you can take pictures of me with it in Hank Aaron's footsteps!"

"And I've got another idea," Kate said. "I'm going to make a copy of Hank's footprints! That way, we'll have a souvenir!"

They ran back to the car. Kate grabbed two pencils and pieces of paper from her mother's notepad while Mike rummaged through the trunk of the rental car, looking for the bat.

"It's not here!" he said.

The only things in the trunk were the two posters in tubes that Oliver had given them yesterday, Mrs. Hopkins's work bag, and two Atlanta sweatshirts they had bought at yesterday's game.

"Where's Big D's bat?" Mike asked. "It was here earlier!"

"Well, I might have an idea," Kate said. She

clenched her hands and pretended to swing a bat. *"¡Déjame golpear primero!"*

Kate was teaching herself Spanish. She liked to try out words and phrases when she remembered them.

"What?" Mike asked.

Kate swung again. "Can I take the first swing if I help you find the bat?"

"I guess so," Mike said. "Where's the bat?"

Kate leaned over and jiggled both poster tubes. Then she picked up one of them and handed it to Mike.

Mike popped the plastic end of the poster tube off and peered inside. Then he tilted the other end of the tube up and held his hand under the open end.

WHOOSH!

The handle of Big D's cracked baseball bat slid into Mike's palm!

Mike stepped in front of Kate. "You put that in there!" he said. "You shouldn't be able to bat first!"

Kate flipped her ponytail and shrugged. "All I know is that your bat was lost and I found it," she said. "Hand it over for my first hit!"

Mike sighed. "Okay," he said as he handed the bat over. "But I'll race you back to the footprints. Go!" Mike took off running.

Mike won the race, but Kate batted first. After that, they took turns standing on Hank Aaron's footprints and pretending to hit home runs while Kate's mom took pictures.

When they were done, Mike and Kate each placed a piece of paper on one of the footprints and rubbed back and forth with the pencils. As they covered the paper with gray shading, the outlines of Hank's footprints emerged in white.

"This is great!" Mike said. "Now we can say we've walked in Hank Aaron's footsteps!"

Kate nodded.

"Okay, time to go," Mrs. Hopkins said. "I've got a little extra work to do before the game, since Tommy Blocks won't be managing today. The team didn't want to take a chance with the threatening note in the display case."

"Is he gone for good?" Kate asked.

"No," Mrs. Hopkins said. "Since they haven't found Hank's bat and ball, they decided the safest thing to do was to have him take some time off."

"Then who's managing the team today?" Mike asked.

"Marty Miller," Mrs. Hopkins said. "The first-base coach."

8

A Secret Message

Half an hour later, Mike and Kate were back at Monument Park in the stadium. Kate's mom had just gone up to the pressroom to work, but they had some time to fill before the game.

"I knew it!" Mike said. "Smarty Marty is up to something! Now he's got Tommy's job!"

Kate nodded. "We don't have enough evidence to prove he did it yet," she said. "But if we find Hank's ball and bat, maybe we'll be able to tell who stole them!"

"The game doesn't start for a couple of hours," Mike said. "Let's check with Jamal and Kayla. Maybe they've learned something new."

It didn't take long for Mike and Kate to get to the security office.

"We don't have any new leads," Jamal said. "We talked to different people and found out that the bat and ball must have been stolen between eleven p.m. and nine a.m. That's the only time that no one was in the room to see the thief."

"But what about Smarty Marty?" Kate asked. "We saw him eating Little Red Herrings, and we found a Little Red Herring at the scene of the crime."

"We interviewed Marty, and he has a solid alibi for the time that the items were stolen," Jamal said. "His partner told us he was home all night. We'll continue to investigate, though."

"How about the key that Oliver used to open the case?" Mike asked. "Has anyone else used it?"

Kayla shook her head. "Nope," she said. "We checked that out thoroughly. It's been locked in the safe in the owner's office. The last time anyone used it was six months ago, just as Oliver said."

"Okay, thanks for the update," Mike said. "We'll keep our eyes open."

Kate and Mike waved goodbye and wound their way through the stadium to the Hank Aaron statue in Monument Park.

"We can't let Hank down," Kate said. "We've got to find his bat and ball!"

"I know," Mike said. "I guess we have to consider other suspects if it's not Smarty Marty. Someone with access to the stadium.

Someone who wants Tommy gone. And someone who has the means to do it."

"Like who?" Kate asked.

"It could be a lot of people," Mike said. "Let's make a list of suspects. Then we can try to investigate each one or cross them off. Do you still have the notepad from yesterday?"

Kate nodded. She took out the pad of paper and pencil that Oliver had given them when they were in his office yesterday.

Mike pointed to the pad. "Okay, put down Smarty Marty, even if we cross him off," he said. "And then the first-base umpire from last night."

Mike glanced over at Kate, but she wasn't writing anything down. He nudged her. "Hey, are you going to write these ideas down?"

Kate stared at the pad for a moment. Then she rubbed her finger back and forth over it.

A broad smile spread across her face.

"You forgot one other suspect," Kate said.

"Who?" Mike asked.

"Oliver!" Kate said. "Here, rub your finger over the pad of paper."

Mike gave her a quizzical look but extended his finger to feel the surface of the pad. It was uneven!

As he pulled his hand away, Kate tapped the paper with the pencil.

"Remember when we visited the Martin Luther King Jr. Historical Park?" she asked.

"Yes, why?" Mike asked.

"Rubbing the footprints there just gave me an idea," Kate said. "Watch this!"

She took the pencil and brushed it lightly back and forth across the middle of the pad.

Slowly, one stroke after another, words began to appear.

has   last
  throw   game
      Hank's

Kate kept brushing the pencil back and forth.

All of a sudden, Mike drew in his breath.

"Oh, wow," he said. "That's amazing!"

Kate pulled the pencil away from the pad. Lines of white writing emerged from Kate's gray pencil strokes:

Tommy has had his last tantrum.
If you don't throw Tommy out of the game for good,
you'll never see Hank's ball and bat again!

Getting a Handle
on Things

Mike took the pad from Kate and looked at it closely. The pencil had colored the paper gray, but the marks that formed the words were still white because they were pressed into the paper.

"That's exactly the same message that was on the note left by the thief!" Mike said. "He must have written the note on this pad! He was pressing down hard, and it left an imprint on the paper."

Mike handed the pad back to Kate.

"That's why I thought of using the pencil to rub it," Kate said. "I saw the dents in the paper but couldn't read what they said."

Kate looked at the pad. "Know what this means?" she asked.

"Mm-hmm." Mike nodded. "I'd say the evidence points to Oliver as the thief!"

"Exactly!" Kate said. "As a former umpire, he has the motive. As the team's historian, he has the means, because he has access to the key. And as a team employee, he has the opportunity to be in the stadium whenever he wants. Now all we have to do is find the missing bat and ball!"

"Well, if Oliver stole Hank's stuff, it might be in his office!" Mike said. "Let's see if we can search it."

"That's easy if he's not there," Kate said. "But what if he is?"

"I have an idea," Mike said. "Follow me!"

Mike and Kate ran through the stadium to the stairway they used the day before. The same security guard was there. Mike explained how he and Kate needed to show Oliver something, and the guard waved them by.

A few moments later, they stood in front of Oliver's office door.

Kate stepped up and rapped her knuckles on it.

There was no answer.

She rapped harder.

Still no answer.

Mike leaned forward and tried the doorknob.

It turned!

Mike shrugged. "He told us to stop by anytime," he said. "We're just stopping by to wait for him!" Mike opened the door and stepped inside with Kate.

They scanned the room, from the bookcase with baseball cards to the Hank Aaron posters on the wall to the piles of paper on Oliver's desk.

"Okay, quick, where would he hide a bat and ball?" Kate asked.

Mike pointed to a table. "How about under that?" he asked.

They scrambled to the back of the room. The large wooden table stood against the wall with papers on it and boxes underneath. Mike and Kate dropped down and slid the boxes to the side.

The space behind the boxes was empty.

"Nope," Kate said. "There's nothing here."

"Nothing where?" asked a voice from the doorway.

Mike's and Kate's hearts raced. They looked at each other and slowly stood up.

Oliver stood in the doorway.

"Oh, hey, it's you two," he said. "What are you doing here?"

Mike took a short breath in. "Um, ah, yesterday you said to stop by anytime," he said.

Oliver stepped closer. "Oh yes, but it's probably best if you're not in my office when I'm not here," he said.

"You're right," Kate said. "Sorry. We were just looking for something that was missing."

Kate turned and gave Mike a quick wink.

"Mike lost his replica Hank Aaron baseball yesterday," she said.

"Yeah, I couldn't find it after the game," Mike said.

"Okay, well, sorry it isn't here," Oliver

said. He walked over to his desk and took some papers. "But I'm afraid I have to lock up, so you'll need to leave. Perhaps you can buy another one upstairs."

"Sure, no problem," Mike said. He nudged Kate. "We'll just take *one last look around* on our way out."

Mike and Kate started walking toward the door, but they took their time to scan the room. With each step, they studied the objects in Oliver's office. The piles of papers and books. Display cases filled with trophies. A box of baseballs on a shelf. Nothing looked big enough to hide a bat behind.

Just before they reached the door, Mike spotted the Hank Aaron posters on the wall.

He stopped suddenly.

His eyes dropped down to the pile of poster tubes at the base of the wall. Then he glanced at the poster tube in front of Oliver's desk. It had SAVE written across the top.

A big smile crossed his face.

Without a word, Mike darted to the desk. He picked up the poster tube leaning against it and popped the white plastic top off.

"Wait," Oliver said from behind the desk. He raised his hands. "Don't touch that!"

Mike didn't listen. Instead, he flipped the tube upside down and held his hand out.

There was a *WHOOSH*!

Hank Aaron's bat dropped into his hand. And Hank's ball slid out of the tube and bounced off the bat!

"Quick, Kate!" Mike yelled. "Call Jamal and Kayla!"

Coach for a Day

The sun was out, but a cool breeze blew through the Atlanta Braves' stadium at the Sunday-afternoon baseball game between Atlanta and Boston.

Mike, Kate, and Mrs. Hopkins were sitting in the first row, just behind the Braves' dugout. It was the first inning of the game, and neither team had scored yet. Mike and Kate had met with Jamal and Kayla before the game while Mrs. Hopkins finished up some work. But now they were just polishing off hot dogs and pretzels.

"So what's happened to Oliver?" Mrs. Hopkins asked.

"He was arrested for theft," Mike answered. "He'll probably have to pay a large fine and do community service. Jamal says that Oliver confessed to it all, after we found the missing items in his office and turned in his notepad that was used to write the message."

"How did he steal Hank's ball and bat?" Mrs. Hopkins asked.

"Apparently, he came in at six a.m. and stole them before anyone else arrived," Kate said.

"What about the display case?" her mother asked. "I thought the key was in the owner's safe."

"When Oliver used it last year, he made a copy of it," Mike said. "He opened the display case with the copied key and used gloves so he wouldn't leave fingerprints. Then he stored the ball and bat in a poster tube in his office. He thought they would be safe there, but I guess he didn't count on us!"

Kate gave Mike a high five.

"And Smarty Marty wasn't involved at all?" Kate's mom asked.

"Nope," Kate said. "Oliver just left the Little Red Herring with the note in the hopes that people would suspect Marty. That's why he used a team notepad to write the note. His motive was to have Tommy fired because he was tired of him being mean to the umpires. Then he was going to return the ball and bat to the team's office. He just didn't count on us two detectives getting involved!"

"Hey, look!" Mike said. "Big D's up!"

Big D walked to the plate. After he adjusted his batting gloves, he scanned the crowd.

When he spotted Mike and Kate, he broke into a broad smile. His eyes twinkled. He pointed at Mike and Kate with his finger and then to right field with his bat. He gave them a nod and stepped into the batter's box.

Mike jumped out of his seat. "He's going to hit a home run for us!" he said. "Just like Babe Ruth's called shot!"

Kate stood up to watch.

The Atlanta pitcher waited for a sign from

his catcher. When he saw it, the pitcher nodded and went into his windup.

The ball flew over home plate.

"STRIKE!" the umpire called.

The pitcher threw a second time.

For a moment it looked like Big D would
let it fly by.

But he didn't.

In a flash, he swung down hard on the ball.
TWAP!

The ball sailed over the infield. Big D dropped his bat and ran for first base. As he passed the Atlanta dugout, he tipped his hat to Mike and Kate.

Mike and Kate cheered him on.

The ball sailed over the field.

Big D rounded first and kept going. He passed second base.

The ball dropped over the right-field fence.

"Woo-hoo!" Mike called. "Big D hit a home run for us!"

The small number of Boston fans in the crowd cheered as Big D crossed home plate and high-fived his teammates.

Mike and Kate sat back down as the game resumed.

Unfortunately for the Boston fans, that was the only hit the Red Sox would get all night. Instead, Atlanta walloped one ball after another as they routed the Red Sox. The Atlanta fans grew so tired of cheering that by the end of the game, they barely even made noise when a player got a hit.

In the end, Atlanta beat Boston eleven to one!

Mike, Kate, and Mrs. Hopkins stood up to leave. It had been a long day. "Oh, I almost forgot," Kate said. "Before we go, Jamal asked that Mike and I stop at the Atlanta dugout after the game. Someone wanted to talk to us."

"Who?" Kate's mom asked.

"I don't know," Kate said. "I guess we'll find out."

They walked to the end of the aisle, near the side of the Atlanta dugout. As they did, Tommy Blocks popped out of the dugout.

"Hello there," he said. Tommy took off his baseball cap. "Mighty nice to see you again.

I hear that I owe you an awful lot for chasing down Hank's stolen slugger and saving my job!"

"We didn't want you or Hank Aaron's bat and ball to disappear," Mike said.

Tommy smiled. "Well, that's good," he said. "I know that I certainly appreciate it!"

Tommy looked down at the ground for a moment and scuffed the concrete floor with his cleats. "This whole thing has helped me

realize that maybe I should be a little nicer to the umpires," he said. "I'm still going to argue with them, but I'll make sure to do it nicely from now on!"

Tommy snapped his fingers. "And that reminds me," he said. "To pay you back, I have an idea."

"What?" Kate asked.

"How would you two like to sit on the bench with me during tomorrow's game and help me coach?" Tommy asked.

"Really?" Mike asked.

"Yes, since you saved my job, it's the least I can do," Tommy said.

"That would be great," Mike said. "But only on one condition."

"What's that?" Tommy asked.

Mike grinned. "You let *me* be the first one to get thrown out of the game!"

Dugout Notes

☆ Atlanta Braves ☆

Remembering Martin. Martin Luther King Jr. is closely connected with Atlanta. At the Martin Luther King Jr. National Historical Park in downtown Atlanta, you can visit the civil rights leader's boyhood home and the Ebenezer Baptist Church, where he and his father were pastors. A museum highlights his leadership in the fight for civil rights. You can also visit his grave site and a reflecting pool.

Misleading red herrings. An important part of any mystery story is a *red herring*. Red herrings are pieces of information that seem important but really aren't, like the gummy candy red herrings in this story. Legend says the name is based on smoked herring fish that might have been used to throw hunting dogs off the scent.

A city of Olympic sports. Atlanta was the host for the 1996 Summer Olympics. Centennial Olympic Park in downtown Atlanta was the main Olympic stadium. It was used for the opening and closing ceremonies and track-and-field events. After the Olympics, it was turned into the Atlanta Braves' new home and renamed Turner Field. They used it from 1997 to 2016, when they moved to a new stadium north of Atlanta.

A drink at the World of Coca-Cola. The famous soft drink Coca-Cola was invented in Georgia in 1886. The recipe is still top-secret, but Atlanta visitors can tour the World of Coca-Cola in downtown Atlanta to learn more about the soft drink's history. You can also sample lots of sodas from around the world, including some very strange-flavored ones!

Combustible Bobby Cox. Tommy Blocks isn't real. But Atlanta's Bobby Cox is. Bobby Cox is one of the Braves' most famous managers. He managed the Braves for twenty-four years, including the year they won the World Series. More importantly for this story, Bobby holds the MLB record for being thrown out of baseball games more than any other manager—158 during the regular season (you can add three ejections during post-season play).

A Presidential visit. The Jimmy Carter Presidential Library and Museum is just outside of Atlanta. It's dedicated to the United States' thirty-ninth president and a longtime Georgia resident, Jimmy Carter. Jimmy was a peanut farmer from Plains, Georgia, who became president in 1977. He has had a long life helping others, such as building houses with Habitat for Humanity. He's the only president so far to live to be older than ninety-four!

A super stadium. The Atlanta Braves currently play

in a stadium a little north of
downtown Atlanta. It opened
in 2017 and has lots of fun fea-
tures, including a rock-climbing
wall, a zip line, and free glove rentals so
kids can try to catch a home run or foul ball!

A whole lot of history. The Atlanta
Braves are the oldest continually operat-
ing baseball team. They started in 1871 as
the Red Stockings in Boston. They went
through many names there (Boston Red
Stockings, Red Caps, Beaneaters, Doves,
Rustlers, Braves, and Bees) and then moved
to Milwaukee as the Braves in 1953. They've
been in Atlanta, as the Braves, since 1966.
They won World Series in 1914, 1957, and
1995—once in each city they've lived in
(Boston, Milwaukee, and Atlanta)!

Lots of Peachtrees. Atlanta has more than seventy roads with *Peachtree* in their names. But the city wasn't named after famous Georgia peaches. Instead, the name came from the Cherokee, who were Atlanta's earliest inhabitants. One of their villages was called Standing Pitch Tree, which later became Peach Tree.

Phantom stadium. The Fulton County Stadium, where Hank Aaron hit home run 715, is both long gone and still here. While the site of the stadium is now a parking lot, the city left up the section of the wall that Hank's ball flew over. The city also embedded the outlines of home plate and the basepaths in the parking lot, so you can re-create Hank's famous home run!

A Note from the Author

Hammerin' Hank Aaron. Hank Aaron was a huge part of my childhood, and I really wanted him to be part of this Atlanta mystery. Not only did he beat Babe Ruth's famous record of 714 home runs when I was in Little League, but I met him the year he did it! He stayed at a hotel near my house before playing in a game at the Baseball Hall of Fame in Cooperstown, New York. I went down to the hotel restaurant during breakfast, and he signed a baseball for me!

But for the game of baseball and fans everywhere, Hank's legacy is much greater than a signature. He endured racism with strength and resilience during his career and while closing on Babe Ruth's home run record, and he became a champion of civil rights on and off the field. His home run record of 755 lasted thirty-three years, but his strength and spirit will be remembered forever.